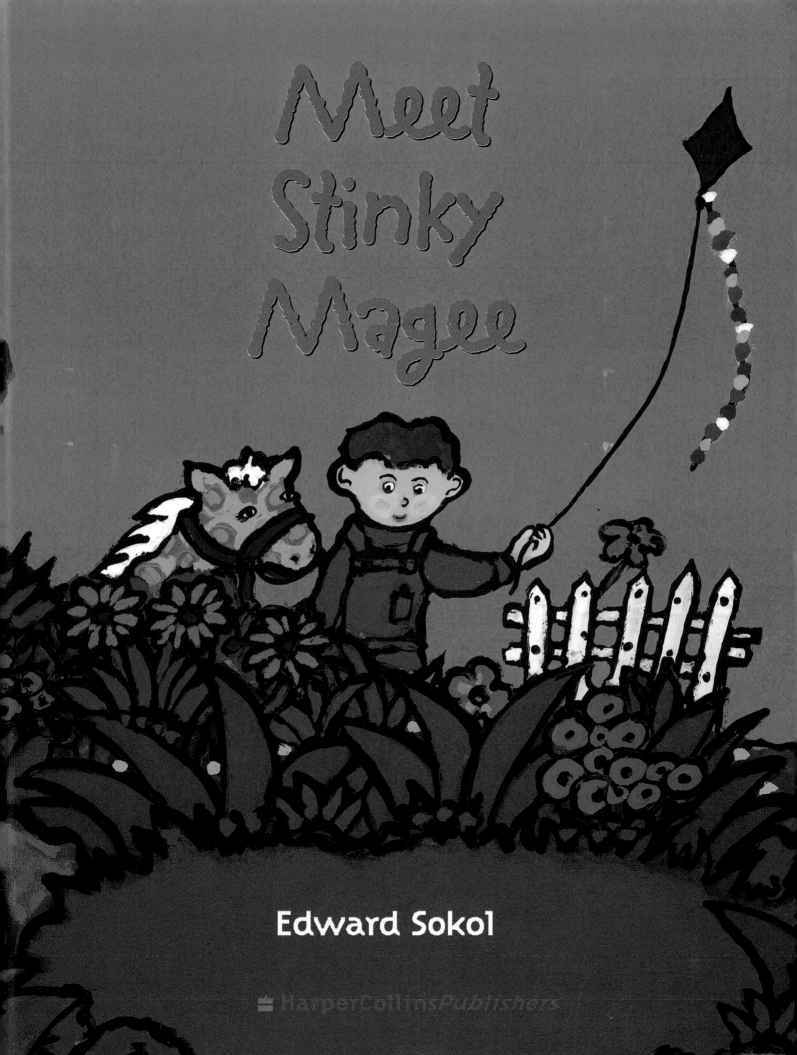

Meet Stinky Magee

Edward Sokol

HarperCollinsPublishers

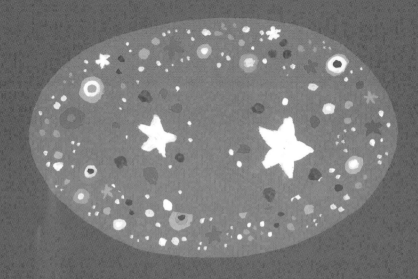

The artist used pen and ink, acrylic and latex paints,
and anything else that
looks interesting to create his mixed-media
full-color illustrations.
The text type is 18-point Citizen font.

Meet Stinky Magee
Copyright © 2000 by Edward Sokol

Printed in Singapore at Tien Wah Press.
All rights reserved.

www.harperchildrens.com

Library of Congress Cataloging-in-Publication Data
Sokol, Edward.
Meet Stinky Magee / by Edward Sokol.
p.   cm.
Summary: Stinky Magee rides his magical hobbyhorse Shnoznik
to their secret land of Snaggarumfrey and has the best
chocolate ice-cream sundae in the world.
ISBN 0-688-17416-7 (trade)—ISBN 0-688-17417-5 (library)
[1. Ice cream, ices, etc.—Fiction. 2. Magic—Fiction.]
I. Title.   PZ7.S68577 Me 2000   [E]—dc21   99-30489

1 2 3 4 5 6 7 8 9 10
◆
First Edition

For my first-grade students at P.S. 150 . . .
who allowed me to share a world of imagination
that I never really left.

With thanks to:
My editor, Barbara Lalicki, for helping this book "grow"
Great advice from BW
Marie Alpert (aka la Contessa), for the fun of it
Judy Kennedy,
for my first professional literary encouragement
Felicie
and
Toni Mendez & Associates

Say hello to Stinky Magee.

He's a funny little guy
with curly orange hair,
green eyes . . .
and big ears that stick out really far.

People say that Stinky looks
just like his grandpa
Captain Silas Hornblower Magee

. . . especially the ears.

Stinky loves to play.
He has a top to spin,

drums to bang on,

a train set that goes round and round,

and lots of other toys.

But his favorite thing in the world
is Shnoopsie, his magic hobbyhorse.

They go everywhere together.

Stinky and Shnoopsie like to travel
to their secret land of Snaggamumfrey,
a place where any wish can come true.

In Snaggamumfrey there are:

giant purple birds
with polka-dot hats,

trees that grow
upside down,

and candy and ice cream that's free

. . . just for the asking.

One day Shnoopsie said to Stinky,
"What would you like to do now?"
Stinky thought for a minute and said,
"I'd like to have the best chocolate
ice-cream sundae in the world."

Shnoopsie said, "Hop on my back,
and I'll take you to Snaggamumfrey.
We can go to the Free Ice Cream Palace.
Just say the magic words, and we'll be off."
Stinky grinned, then shouted,
"Be good, be fast . . . be gone!"

They flew so fast, they flew so high,
they almost touched the top of the sky.

Stinky yelled with glee,
"Snaggamumfrey, here we come!"

The moon and the sun and the stars

twinkled around them.

Soon they saw the Free Ice Cream Palace.
The sign had lights all around it
in red and blue and green and white.

With a whoosh and a plop,
they landed at the front door.
Then they went inside.

The waiter Maurice said,
"Hello, Mr. Stinky. We've been expecting you.
What is it you wish to eat?"

Stinky said, "All I wish is one delicious,
ooey-gooey, slightly chewy,
messy, smudgy, chocolate fudgy,
sweet and dreamy, real whip creamy
extra-special ice-cream sundae
. . . with a bright red,
really red cherry on top!"

Before you could say, "Peep, pop, tiddle-op,"
the chocolate sundae appeared
in front of Stinky.

He ate the fudge, he ate the cream
and all the layers in between.

He ate and ate, and had such fun
. . . he didn't stop 'til he was done

. . . but he left the bright red,
really red cherry 'til the very end.

At last he popped it in his mouth.
"Yippee!" said Stinky.

Shnoopsie whispered,
"Stinky, we have to get you home to bed.
We've been gone a long time."

Stinky said to Maurice,
"Thank you, sir, for the extra-delicious
ice-cream sundae."

Stinky hopped onto Shnoopsie
and shouted the magic words,
"Be good, be fast . . . be gone!"
They flew home to Puddingtown.

Stinky must have fallen asleep
on the way home. When he opened his eyes,
he was in his pajamas in bed.

He looked at Shnoopsie and said,
"I had so much fun eating
my ooey-gooey ice-cream sundae.
What ever will we do on Monday?"

Shnoopsie winked at Stinky and said,
"We can do anything you wish!"